For Rebecca, my wife and best friend.–A.C.
For my parents, Sara and Emilio. Matthew 6:21.–D.S.

Copyright Text©1990 Andrew Clements.
Illustrations©1990 Debrah Santini.
Published by Picture Book Studio, Saxonville, MA.
Distributed in Canada by Vanwell Publishing, St. Catharines, Ont.
All rights reserved.
Printed in Hong Kong.
10 9 8 7 6 5 4 3 2 1

Library of Congress Cataloging in Publication Data
Clements, Andrew, 1949-
Santa's secret helper / by Andrew Clements ; illustrated by Debrah Santini.
Summary: One Christmas Eve Santa has a secret helper who sets off in a
reindeer-drawn sleigh with a huge sack of toys, just like Santa. But who
is it? And will the helper do the job as well as Santa?
ISBN 0-88708-136-3: $14.95
1. Santa Claus–Juvenile fiction. [1. Santa Claus–Fiction.]
I. Santini, Debrah, ill. II. Title.
PZ7.C59118San   1990
[E]–dc20   90-8601

Ask your bookseller for these other Picture Book Studio books by Andrew Clements:
Big Al illustrated by Yoshi
Noah & the Ark & the Animals illustrated by Ivan Gantschev
And this one illustrated by Debrah Santini:
The Baby Who Would Not Come Down by Joan Knight

Andrew Clements

SANTA'S SECRET HELPER

Debrah Santini

Picture Book Studio

It was two days before Christmas, and all of Santa's elves were especially busy. They were really twice as busy as usual, because this year there are two sleighs to pack, two Santa suits to clean and mend, two pairs of black boots to shine, and two teams of reindeer to be fed and rested and ready.

Why two of this and two of that and two of the other when there is only one Santa? Because this year Santa has a secret helper.

On Christmas Eve Santa and his secret helper are all
ready to leave with their big sacks of toys and treats.
It's even hard for the elves to tell which one is the real
Santa. And as the sun goes down, two sleighs take
off—one to the east and one to the west.

Will anyone be able to tell that one Santa is just a helper?

The secret helper flies to the first rooftop and pops down the chimney. After putting presents under the tree and stuffing little toys and candy canes into each stocking, the helper eats the cookies and drinks the milk that the children have left for Santa, and leaves a little note that says, "Thank you."
That's just what Santa would have done.

The secret helper sees a lost puppy in the snow. Before too long that puppy has been left in a cozy basket by a fireplace where only one stocking is hanging from the mantel. The puppy and one little child will each find a wonderful new friend on Christmas morning.
That's just what Santa would have done.

The reindeer get a little tired, so the secret helper lets them rest. They stop at a crèche in front of a church and the animals eat some of the hay that is there on the ground. This is a kind and thoughtful thing to do, and that's just what Santa would have done.

A mother and father who are still awake open their
bedroom window to wave and call out, "Hello! Hello,
Santa!" The helper calls back, "Why hello there–
Merry Christmas, Merrrry Christmas!" and gives
them a happy wave.
That's just what Santa would have done.

At the very last house, the secret helper is extra quiet. It is almost morning, and even a little noise might wake the children before everything is ready. The helper whisks back up the chimney, and soon the sleigh with the empty toy sack is speeding through the gray sky, headed north.

Back home at last, the helper puts the sleigh away carefully, and hangs up the harness on the wall of the barn. Soon all the reindeer are munching their hay and Christmas oats.

The secret helper goes into the house and takes off the big white beard, and the big black boots, and the red and white Santa suit, and puts on some night clothes and a warm robe and slippers.

And then the secret helper gives the real Santa a great big hug. And look who it is… it's Mrs. Claus, Santa's own best friend! She's having the most wonderful Christmas.

Santa wants his wife to tell him all about her trip, but she's ready to take a long winter's nap after her busy night.

And so she takes off her robe, puts
on her nightcap, and lies down
and pulls up the covers. Then she
closes her eyes, says her prayers,
and goes to sleep.

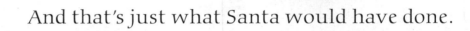

And that's just what Santa would have done.